Real-Life CRIMES

... and how they were solved

Andrei Chikatilo
The Red Ripper
Murder in Hollywood
A Double Killing

UK £1.50 Republic of Ireland IR£1.75 Malta M£1.25

Real-Life CRIMES

... and how they were solved

Contents

Volume 7 Part 94

COMING IN PART 95

CRIME CASE STUDY

"I Didn't Kill My Babies": In 1965 police investigated the disappearance of two children. Their mother said they had vanished from their room. But officers thought she was hiding something

MIND OF EVIL

Killed For Their Cash: Eugen Weidmann had been in trouble most of his life. But in 1937 he started on a brutal killing spree in France– murdering his victims for their money

INCRIMINATING EVIDENCE

Death of a Diamond Dealer: London jeweller Leo Grunhut was shot dead on his own doorstep in 1978. But the case remained unsolved until 1990, when an interesting story was uncovered

Published by:
Eaglemoss Publications Ltd
7 Cromwell Road
London SW7 2HR
Circulation Manager:
Gary Neale
Subscription and Back Numbers Enquiries:
Customer Services 0424 755755

Editorial offices:
REAL-LIFE CRIMES
Midsummer Books Ltd
179 Dalling Road
London W6 0ES

Managing Editor: Stan Morse
Editors: Chris Bishop
John Monks
Trisha Palmer
Production Editor: Sheryl Fellows
Design: Sharon Whittaker
Picture Researchers: Veneta Bullen
Davina Bullen
Sophie Mortimer

Colour reproduction:
Chroma Graphics Pte Ltd, Singapore
Printed in Great Britain by: BPC Magazines Ltd

HOW TO MAKE SURE YOUR COLLECTION IS COMPLETE

To be sure of getting your copies each week, either place a regular order with your newsagent or take out a subscription.

ARE YOU MISSING ANY COPIES?

Back numbers are usually available, at cover price, from your local newsagent.

In case of difficulty in any of the following countries, write to the addresses below, marking your envelope REAL-LIFE CRIMES Back Numbers. Enclose a cheque or postal order, made payable to the appropriate company, for the cover price x the number of copies you want (e.g. 4 copies x £1.50 = £6.00; postage and package are free). Please remember to specify which issue numbers you want.

UK and Republic of Ireland: Woodgate (Eaglemoss) Ltd, PO Box 1, Hastings, TN35 4TJ

Australia: Your nearest branch of Gordon and Gotch Ltd.

Malta: Miller Distributors Ltd, PO Box 272, MA, Vasselli Street, Valletta

BINDERS

UK and Republic of Ireland: Binders are priced at £5.95/IR£5.95. To get your binder, send a cheque or postal order, made payable to Woodgate (Eaglemoss) Ltd, to REAL-LIFE CRIMES Binders, PO Box 1, Hastings, TN35 4TJ. For payment by credit card, telephone 0424 755755.

Australia: Binders are priced at $14.95. To get your binder, send a cheque or money order, made payable to Bissett Magazine Services Pty Ltd, to REAL-LIFE CRIMES Binders, PO Box 315, Vermont, Victoria, or telephone (03) 872 4000.

ACKNOWLEDGEMENTS

Authors: Ray Granger
Patrick Pender

Photography: David Hendley
Richard Gibson

For their valuable help and advice, our thanks to:

Emeritus Professor Alan Usher

Picture acknowledgements

Front cover: via Flegon Press. **2055:** via Flegon Press (all). **2056-2060:** via Flegon Press (all). **2061:** John Frost Newspapers/via Flegon Press/via Flegon Press. **2062-2063:** via Flegon Press. **2064:** John Frost Newspapers/via Flegon Press. **2065:** Sipa Press-Rex Features/via Flegon Press/via Flegon Press. **2066:** Jonathan Goodman/Midsummer. **2067:** Range-Bettmann-UPI/Range-Bettmann-UPI. **2068-2069:** Range-Bettmann-UPI. **2070:** Range-Bettmann-UPI/Range-Bettmann-UPI. **2071:** The Kobal Collection/Midsummer. **2072:** Syndication International/Photo News Old Bailey/Photo News Old Bailey. **2073:** Photo News Old Bailey. **2074:** Enterprise News & Pictures (all). **2075:** Enterprise News & Pictures/Photo News Old Bailey. **2076:** John Frost Newspapers/Enterprise News & Pictures.

THE RED RIPPER

Andrei Chikatilo was a model Soviet citizen: a hard-working Party member, a former Russian literature teacher and a loving, softly-spoken grandfather. But he was also a serial killer who, during a 12-year murder spree, committed vile acts of unparalled ferocity, depravity and barbarism.

ANDREI CHIKATILO

Chikatilo's victims were children or young women who were lured to deserted spots and repeatedly stabbed and mutilated, usually around the genital area and the eyes.

Andrei Chikatilo's 'secret house' was little more than a hut with a bed and some basic pieces of furniture. Initially he took prostitutes there, but before long he turned his attention to young girls.

Andrei Chikatilo probably did not have murder on his mind when he began talking to the chubby little girl by the tram stop. He knew he had what he called a "sexual weakness"; he liked to kiss and fondle children, but he had never harmed one.

It was the shortest day of the year, 22 December 1978, and although not yet six o'clock it was already dark. The girl, Lena Zakotnova, had gone skating after school and was now on her way home. However, after just a few minutes talking to the tall, stooped man with the kindly manner, she trotted off behind him.

Chikatilo did not head home to his family apartment on Fifty Years of the All-Union Leninist-Communist Youth League

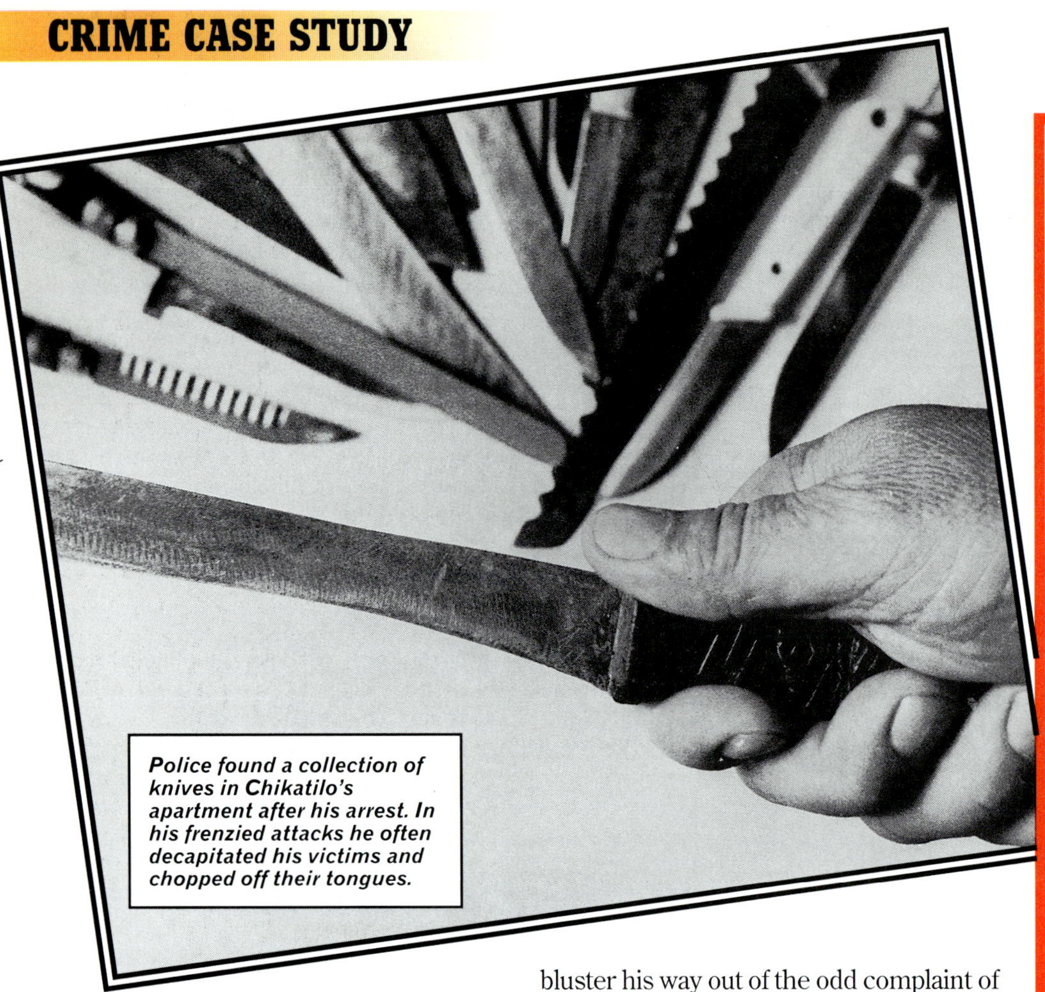

Police found a collection of knives in Chikatilo's apartment after his arrest. In his frenzied attacks he often decapitated his victims and chopped off their tongues.

Young lives cut short...

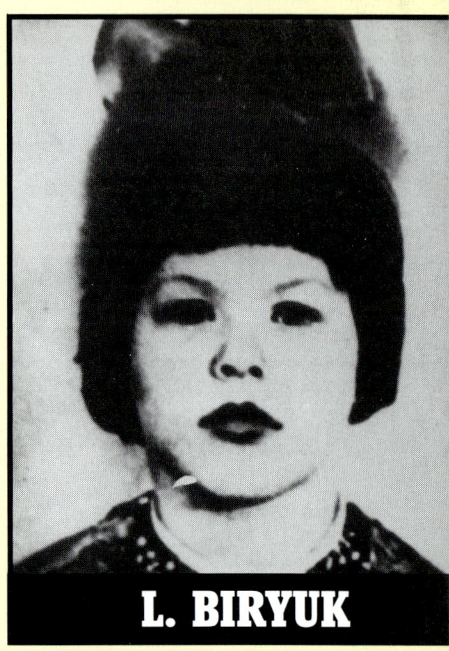

L. BIRYUK

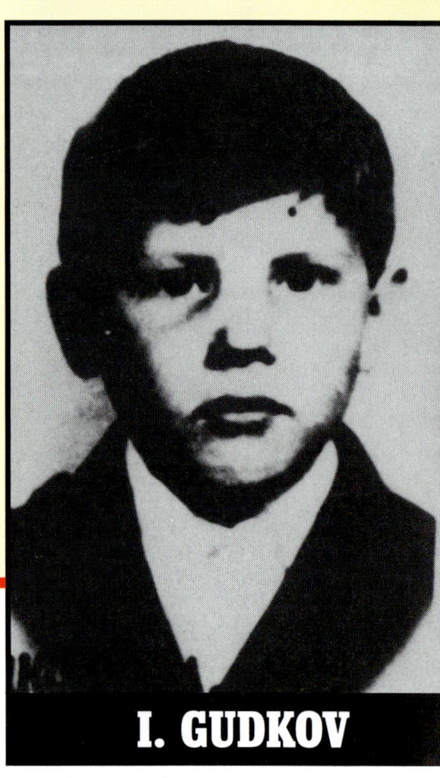

I. GUDKOV

Street in Shakhti, a grim mining community in southern Russia, but to a three-roomed stucco shack on the other side of town at 26 Border Lane. He had bought it secretly, for just 1,500 rubles, earlier that year as somewhere to take prostitutes. He nursed a special craving, though, for little girls, for the sense of power they gave him.

Once they were through the front door, he locked it, flicked on the light and pounced on Lena, throwing her to the ground and tearing at her winter clothing. When she began to scream he put his arm across her throat until she lost consciousness and then wrapped her scarf around her head as a blindfold.

Sexual frenzy

He could not rape the helpless girl; although capable of excitement and orgasm, he had never managed a proper erection. He had fathered his two children only by using his fingers to put his semen 'where it belonged'. This time, in his frenzy, he tore roughly at the girl's genitals. The sight of blood filled him with an excitement he had never felt before.

He took a knife from his bag – he had been carrying it for a few weeks as the older boys at the school where he taught had started beating him up – and began stabbing the girl in the stomach. When he had finished he realised that he was in big trouble; an active party member, a university graduate and a teacher, he could bluster his way out of the odd complaint of child molesting, but not this.

Carrying the girl – who was still alive but unconscious – under one arm, he left the house, crossed a patch of waste ground opposite and threw her into a stream, tossing her school bag after her. Although Chikatilo was questioned after the murder – spots of blood had been found in the snow near his house – another local man was arrested.

Second victim

In March 1981 Chikatilo left teaching – his weakness had got the better of him once too often – and found a clerical job in an engineering factory. His new work required him to travel around the region – and sometimes further afield – to track down supplies. Later that year, in the evening of 3 September, he met a young woman in Rostov, the nearest big city. Seventeen-year-old Larissa Tkachenko went to school in Rostov and lived on a collective farm outside the city.

Although she wasn't a professional prostitute, she was a wild girl who regularly absconded from her dormitory to spend the evening with local soldiers. When Chikatilo approached her, she willingly went with him across the Don and along the river to a forest area that was a traditional trysting place for courting couples. He tried to have sex with her, but failed again. She mocked him, and in his fury he strangled her, punching her in the face and forcing dirt into her mouth. He did not have a knife with him, so he began to bite the girl. When he'd finished he mutilated her vagina with a stick, then wiped his bloodied hands and mouth on her clothes. Before he left he covered her body with newspapers.

There was no turning back for Chikatilo now. He knew that he could only really get sexual pleasure from using violence, from beating, stabbing and biting. He knew he would kill again.

His third victim, Lyuba Biryuk, aged 13, died in June 1982. She was walking home

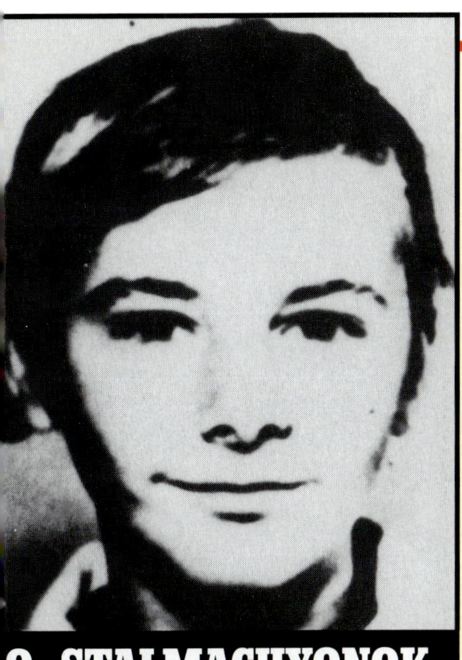

O. STALMACHYONOK

hikatilo preyed on the vulnerable – ostitutes, vagrants, runaways and, articularly, children, who could be easily on over by offers of help or gifts. Lyuba iryuk (pictured left) was walking home om a shopping trip when Chikatilo proached her.

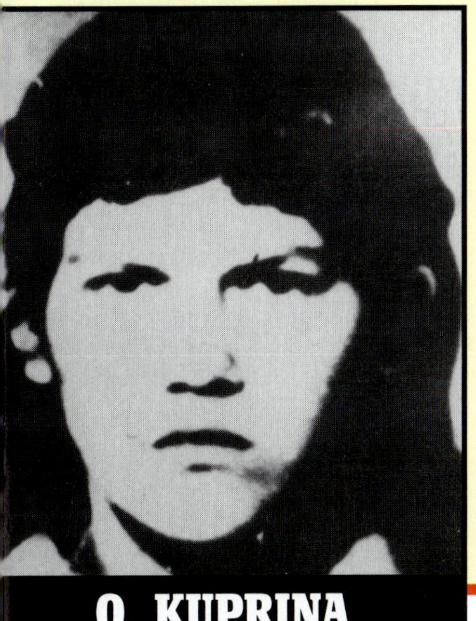

O. KUPRINA

from a shopping trip in a nearby village when Chikatilo fell into step beside her. They chatted, and the killer did not make his move until the path wound through some bushes out of sight of the road. This time he had brought a knife.

On the hunt

Chikatilo started to actively hunt victims, trying to strike up conversations with them and lure them away to a secluded place in a wood or park. He used his Party connections to get the keys to empty apartments, where he would clean up and change his clothes before going home. He also cleaned up the scene after a killing.

He killed six more times in 1982, including two boys. There were eight victims in 1983. By September 1984 he had killed 15 more. Even the Soviet authorities, who officially denounced sex killings as a capitalist crime unknown in the USSR, were forced to admit that there was a serial killer on the loose, although the murders received little press coverage. The Rostov police force, under pressure, set about beating confessions out of various mentally-defective young men, but some officers remained on the alert.

On the evening of 13 September 1984 Inspector Zanasovski saw Chikatilo acting suspiciously in the city's bus station. He had already questioned him, some weeks before, and the name – an unusual one in that part of the world – had stuck in his mind.

The police officer set out with a colleague to follow him. They watched for hours as Chikatilo wandered around the city, getting on and off buses, sitting in the park, and then spending the early hours in the railway station. Everywhere he went he tried to strike up conversations with women on their own, moving from one to another relentlessly. By 6 a.m. he was in the city's marketplace, and still appeared to be searching for someone.

Zanasovski moved in and arrested him on a public morals charge. When Chikatilo's briefcase was searched the police found a kitchen knife with a plastic handle and an eight-inch blade, some lengths of rope and a jar of Vaseline. Chikatilo was questioned, but insisted he had nothing to do with any murders.

Police suspicions

Although their suspicions were strong, the authorities had only one piece of hard evidence about the murderer. Semen samples had been taken from some of the victims. At this time, before genetic fingerprinting, all that could be revealed from these was the killer's blood type, group AB. A sample of Chikatilo's blood was

Background

Steppes of murder

The majority of Chikatilo's crimes were committed in and around Rostov-on-Don, a city of around a million people in the south of Russia. It's essentially a frontier city – locals see the River Don (below) as the boundary between Europe and Asia – and has always had a high crime rate. But it has also enjoyed some periods of prosperity, which have left a legacy of fine buildings, as well as parks and a large botanical garden where Chikatilo killed more then once.

The surrounding countryside is generally flat and windswept and the Soviet regime instructed many pieces of woodland to be planted to act as windbreaks and improve farming conditions.

Bleak towns

The other towns in the region tend to be rather bleak, functional places. Shakhti, where Chikatilo lived when he began killing, is fairly typical. The town's name means 'mines', and the low, uniform houses are dominated by slag heaps.

Below: Nineteen-year-old Vera Shevkyn was killed on 27 October 1983. She was a prostitute and alcoholic, and was picked up by Chikatilo on a housing estate near the mining town of Shakhti.

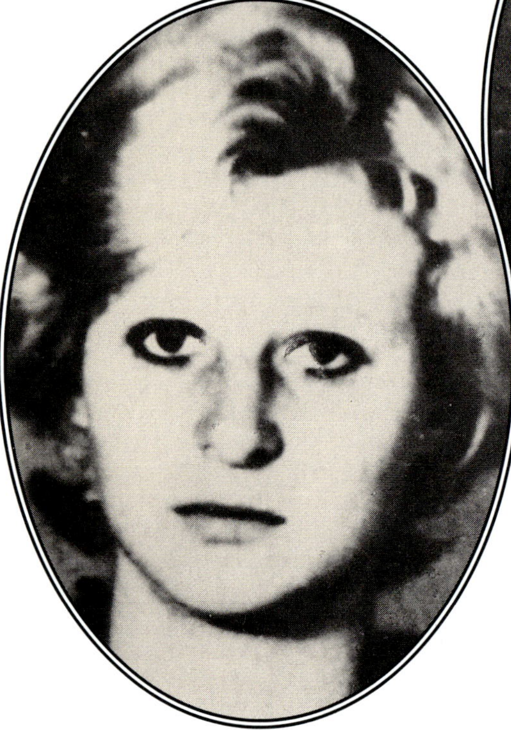

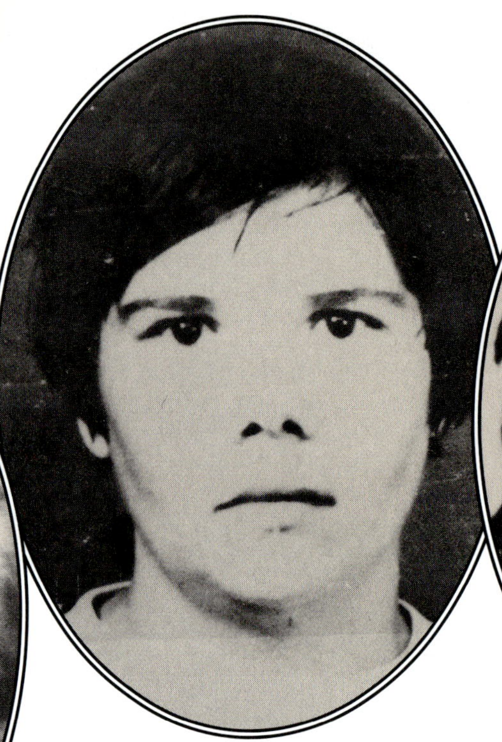

Tanya Petrosan (above left) and her daughter Sveta (above) were murdered on 25 May 1984 while on a picnic with Chikatilo in woods near Shakhti. The 32-year-old former lover of Chikatilo made the mistake of mocking his impotence, and he slaughtered Tanya and then her child as she played nearby.

taken for comparison; it was group A. Reluctantly, the police eliminated him from the enquiry. As a result, whenever his name came up as part of the investigation in future he was discounted.

However, Chikatilo did not go free. There was an outstanding warrant against him for stealing state property – he had taken a car battery from the factory where he worked – and he spent three months in prison. More importantly to him, he was expelled from his beloved Communist Party.

When he was released he set about finding another job, and got one – again working as a supply clerk – in a factory in Novocherkassk, between Rostov and Shakhti. The Chikatilo family moved again. By this time the Soviet central government had become alarmed at what was happening in the Rostov area. In November 1985 Chief Inspector Issu Kostoev of the Department for Crimes of Special Importance was sent to lead the hunt for the serial killer. His first act was to free the young men who had been framed by the Rostov police, and then he set about finding the killer.

As there were no real clues – a partial footprint, together with the angle and force of some of the knife blows suggested the killer was a big man, several witnesses said he wore glasses and the semen was type AB – the hunt was a matter of elimination.

Kostoev outlined several categories of

An ordinary citizen

Andrei Chikatilo was born on 16 October 1936 to a poor peasant family in the village of Yablochnoye in the Ukraine. The area was in the midst of a famine, which had been largely engineered by Josef Stalin.

Both Andrei and his sister, Tatyana, remembered their mother telling them when they were young that they had had an elder brother (or perhaps cousin), Stepan, who had been kidnapped and eaten by starving neighbours. Whether this was true or not – there were no records of a Stepan Chikatilo – there were plenty of horrors around as Andrei grew up, particularly as the German army and the Ukrainian resistance were involved in a bloody guerrilla war all around him.

Painfully shy

Andrei grew into a tall, strong, athletic, but pitifully shy, young man, too shortsighted to see the blackboard at school, but too scared to ask for glasses. He rarely socialised, and threw himself into his studies. As a result, he won a place at a technical college, and was also accepted into the Communist Party.

He was a handsome young man, if a little effeminate, but had no luck with the opposite sex. Although he could satisfy himself, he was impotent with young women. He felt cheated, less than a man, and became paranoid that talk about his inadequacy would get back to his few friends.

Three years in the Red Army left him feeling no better about himself. Strait-laced, sober and virtually humourless, he sought solace in political activity, work and study. He was an inveterate reader of newspapers, and talked politics with anyone who would listen. After the army he found work as a telephone engineer and settled in a small town north of Rostov.

In 1963 Chikatilo married Fenya, who had been introduced to him by his sister. He was still unable to sustain an erection, but managed to father two children, a girl and a boy, of whom he was very fond.

Determined to better himself, he took a correspondence course and got a degree in Russian from Rostov University. Then he began working as a schoolteacher. He went from town to town and from job to job, as he had two basic problems: he was a useless teacher, totally unable to maintain order, and he could not keep his hands off his pupils, boys or girls.

Teaching career ends

In 1978 the Chikatilo family moved to Shakhti, where he bought the shanty at 26 Border Lane. After three years various sexual misdemeanours led to him losing his job at Technical School 33 and he began a new career as a supply clerk in a factory in Shakhti.

His family never suspected him of the murders; he effectively lived a double life. All through the 1980s he had access to various empty apartments via Party and other contacts, where he could rest, wash and change his clothes after a killing. After Chikatilo's arrest his family were given new names and relocated by the state.

Andrei Chikatilo's guise as an ordinary family man helped him escape detection for 12 years. There was nothing to suggest that the kindly grandfather in this happy family photo was the butcher who terrorised a nation.

people on whom to concentrate. These included those with convictions for sex crimes, psychiatric patients and drug addicts; railway workers and car owners (many of the killings were in out-of-the-way places); employees of cultural, educational, athletic and pre-school institutions (the killer showed signs of intelligence and the ability to talk with children); owners of video equipment, who might have used it to lure children away; ex-policemen, slaughter-house workers and even surgeons – the killer was showing a degree of anatomical skill. Card index boxes began to pile up – there was no computer capacity available to the police– and more than 1,000 other crimes, including 95 murders, were solved, but Kostoev's team got no further in their hunt for the serial killer.

Chikatilo killed many of his victims in isolated forests, where their bodies would lie undetected during the long winter months.

Murdered in Moscow

On 1 August 1985 the body of an 18-year-old girl was found at an airport in Moscow. It bore all the hallmarks of the Rostov killer. At the end of the month another 18-year-old was found murdered in Shakhti. Clearly, the killer could move fairly freely about the Soviet Union, which was not always easy.

After this there were no more murders for nearly two years. Kostoev wondered if his quarry had killed himself, or was in prison for other offences. Perhaps he was just lying low, alarmed at all the police activity. Patrols and surveillance had been stepped up in what was now known as Operation Forest Path.

In fact, Chikatilo had been badly shaken by his arrest and questioning. He had killed three boys in 1987, but always while on business trips far from home. The following year he returned to the Rostov region, killing an unknown woman near the town of Krasny Sulin in April.

A little girl died in the Ukraine in May and a 15-year-old boy, Zhenya Muratov, was slaughtered in the woods near a country railway station called Donleshkhoz – Forest Farm. This was little more than a halt, with two bare concrete platforms and a simple shelter for passengers, but it suited Chikatilo perfectly.

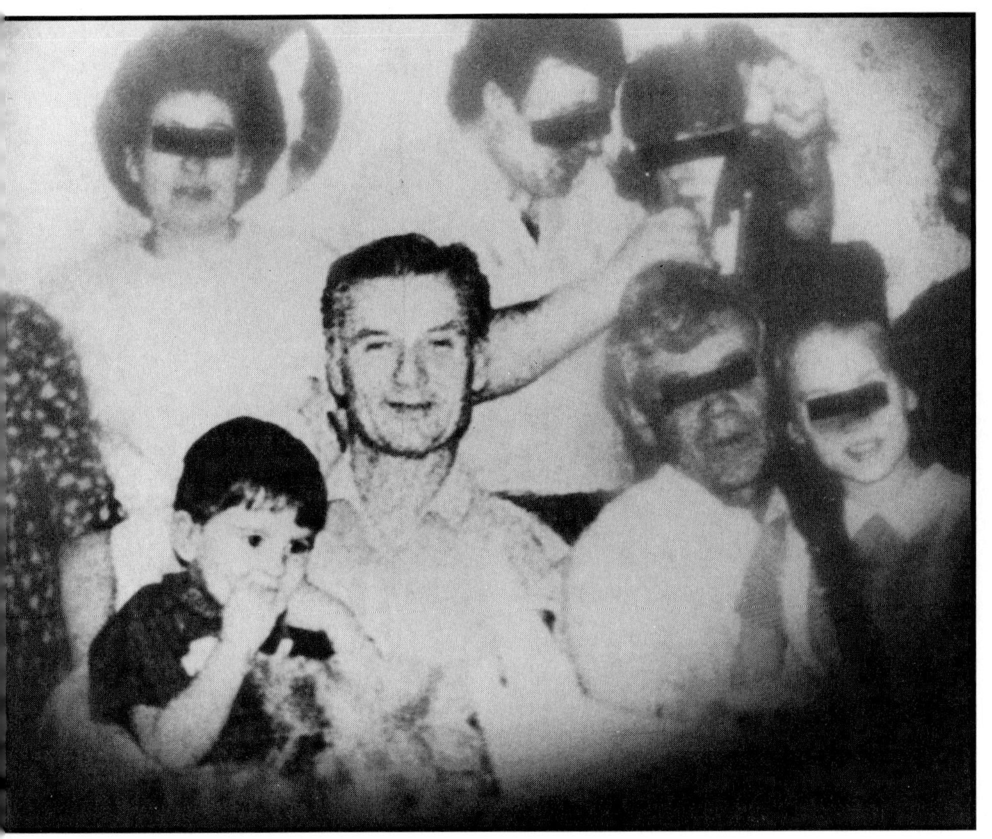

In March 1989 he varied his pattern, killing indoors for the first time since 1978. His daughter and her husband had recently divorced, and he had taken on the task of selling their flat for them. He was not trying too hard, though; it was good to have a secret place of his own.

Teenage runaway

Tanya Ryzhova, 16, a drunken runaway, probably was not the first person he took there. This one, though, began to scream, and he stabbed her in the mouth to silence her. He then went into a frenzy, and was left with a body to dispose of. He dismembered it in the flat, mopped up and went outside to look for a sled.

After loading the body pieces, wrapped in the girl's clothing, onto the sled, he pulled it through the dark, snowbound streets towards the railway, where he hid the bloody parcels in a drain. They were found nine days later.

The police redoubled their efforts patrolling the railways; Kostoev was increasingly convinced that they were the key to solving the murders. With the new openness in the country as Communism crumbled away, publicity about the murders increased, and the police toured local schools warning children against strangers. Nevertheless, there were four more victims that summer – three of them boys – though only two were linked to the manhunt.

Confident killer

In 1990 Chikatilo, growing more confident of eluding the police presence on the trains, began killing more frequently. He had a new job in Rostov that gave him even more time to be away from home. He returned again to his favourite locations, killing once in Shakhti, twice in Rostov's Botanical Gardens and, in April, in the woods near Forest Farm station.

On 14 August Chikatilo murdered a little boy near Novocherkassk's River Beach, where hundreds of people were making the most of a heatwave, and on 17 October, the day after his 54th birthday, he lured 16-year-old Vadim Gromov to Forest Farm. At the end of the month he killed another 16-year-old in Shakhti, and on 6 November he went back to Forest Farm station with 22-year-old Sveta Korostik.

When he returned to the station he was alone. Sergeant Rybakov had been standing on the drab concrete platform for some hours. Following the discovery of Gromov's body in a stand of acacia trees just beyond the station, the police presence on the railway had been stepped up. They were on the trains and on every station between Rostov and Shakhti.

It was typically grey November weather, and the only people Rybakov had seen on the rural station were mushroom-pickers. He was immediately struck by the new arrival. There was a smear of red on his cheek that may have been berry juice, while the mud on his boots and the leaves tangled in his clothes suggested he had gone deeper into the forest than the others. His half-open bag revealed not mushrooms, but a change of clothing.

Police close in on Chikatilo

Rybakov stepped forward and asked to see the man's papers. Chikatilo gave his name and said he was visiting a friend who lived nearby. The policeman handed back the papers and waved him onto the train that had just come in. Something about Chikatilo worried Rybakov, though, and he filed a report about his suspicions.

On 13 November Kostoev and members of his team went to Forest Farm to follow up the murder of Vadim Gromov, and found the body of a young blonde woman half-buried under a pile of leaves and a light covering of snow. Kostoev was beside himself with rage. He had saturated the railway network with policemen and yet his quarry had evaded them all to kill again in a place that could only really be reached by train.

He summoned officers from the local station, who told him about Rybakov's report. As they were talking a passing detective heard the unusual name and said: "We had a man named Chikatilo here in 1984."

Kostoev checked the file. The more he

HE is the most sadistic and perverted killer the world has known.

And as Andrei Romanovich Chikatilo sits smiling and shackled in the iron cage that protects him from the families of his victims, one question is being asked in his home town.

How on earth did we give birth to this monster?

Neighbours and colleagues in Rostov on Don remember the 56-year-old ex-teacher as a kindly and respectable pillar of this quiet, prosperous community in Southern Russia. But a fascinating picture is starting to emerge of the man who ...s confessed to the unspeakable torture and ...g of 55 boys and girls he lured to woods on ...dge of town.

...rding to his psychiatrist, Alexander ...sky, Chikatilo has inhabited a fantasy ...oyhood. By the time he reached 40, ...eep that the only way he could ...sfaction was through the can- ... that have shocked th...

The Chikatilo case made headline news around the world. Many press reports focused on psychiatric records about Chikatilo's feelings of resentment against a hostile world.

Ripper's signature

By the end of 1982 Chikatilo had established a pattern of killing from which he rarely deviated. His victims were girls, young women and, increasingly, boys. The women were usually down-and-outs or prostitutes. Many of the youngsters were runaways or slightly retarded. He picked several of them up at bus stops and train stations, offering to show them short cuts, rare stamps or coins, or a video, or to give them some food and drink; anything to make them come with him. He never used force or got too persuasive, for fear of attracting attention.

Lured to their deaths

He would then lead them to a wooded area, where he would pounce and overpower them. His victims usually died of multiple stab wounds, 30 to 50 in most cases, although some were strangled or battered to death. He always used a knife on the eyes – the police theory was that he believed the eyes of a dead person retain the image of the last thing they saw – and the abdomen, which he sometimes slit open, or covered with a network of wounds.

The female victims had their nipples sliced or bitten off, and Chikatilo usually took the uterus; he liked to chew on it, and rhapsodised to detectives and psychiatrists about its springy texture. He took the penis and testicles of his male victims, which he claimed to have thrown away later, and bit or cut off the tips of their tongues.

Mutilation of bodies

He tended to remove the upper lips and noses of his later victims and put them somewhere else in the body. At first, most of these mutilations were carried out after he had killed his victims, or bludgeoned them unconscious. As time went on, and he got more confident with the knife, he increasingly carried out his gruesome work on live victims, skilfully dodging the spurts of blood; many of them died of shock.

When he finished, he meticulously cleaned up and partially covered the body, either with dead leaves or with newspapers. He generally took away all the victim's clothes and belongings and dumped them somewhere else.

Below: This male victim had his abdomen split open, but unlike in other killings Chikatilo left the genitals intact. These ghoulish operations led police to assume that the murders had been carried out by a weird satanic cult or a gang collecting organs for transplant.

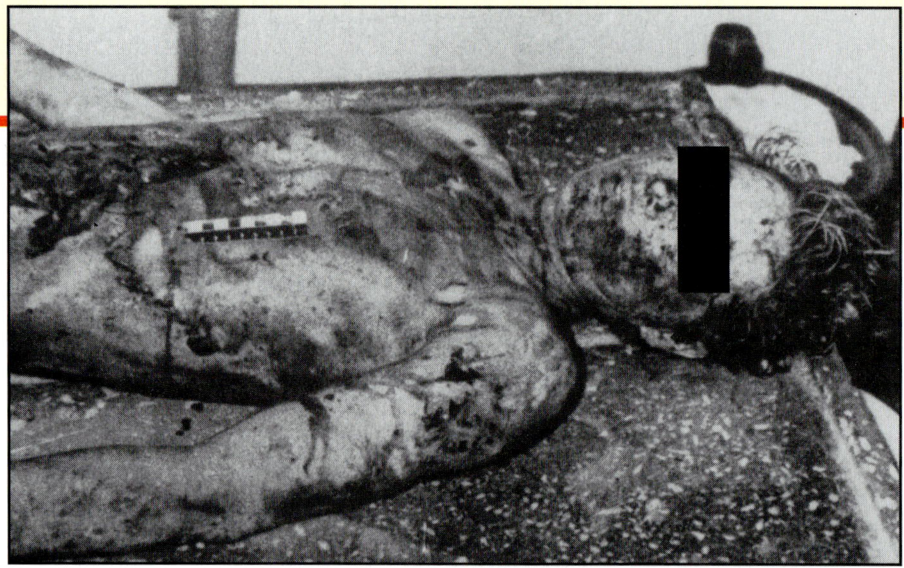

Daily Mail
18 April 1992

omrade Cannibal's rrible revenge on world he thought as against him

read, the more he thought the long search might be over. The labs may have made a mistake. Chikatilo was put under close surveillance by expert KGB officers and was followed every day from his apartment in Novocherkassk to the factory in Rostov. His shadows noted how, on buses and trains, he always sat next to young women and boys and chatted to them. If they rebuffed him, he simply moved along and tried again.

Other officers approached his employers and found that job changes and business trips had put him in the vicinity of all of the murder scenes in the region, and a few others further afield.

Kostoev was convinced. On the afternoon of 20 November three plainclothes policemen walked up to Chikatilo as he stood outside a cafe in Novocherkassk. They asked him his name, then grabbed his arms, handcuffed him and bundled him into a Lada.

Kostoev interrogated his prisoner in the former KGB prison in Rostov. Under Russian law he had 10 days before he had to charge his suspect or set him free. At first Chikatilo was cool and indifferent; he had been questioned about these crimes before, and cleared. Why was he being held again?

Confession vital

Kostoev knew that he wouldn't be believed if he promised a light sentence in exchange for a confession, so he appealed to Chikatilo's vanity and arrogance, telling him he had all the evidence he needed but did not know why he had done it. He mentioned the possibility that Chikatilo would be found insane.

Chikatilo denied everything, including the fact that he had been at Donleskhoz on 6 November. Caught in this lie, he made a statement admitting nothing specific but claiming a history of mental illness. By the eighth day Kostoev thought Chikatilo was ready to crack after he had made another statement asking for treatment. Kostoev brought in a local psychiatrist, Aleksandr Bukhanovsky, to reassure Chikatilo that he would get help in coming to terms with his problems, and then formally charged him with 36 murders.

Chikatilo disclaimed two of them, but admitted the rest and confessed to many others throughout the Soviet Union that had either not been reported or not linked to the other murders. There were 55 in all.

Chikatilo's trial began in Rostov on 14 April 1992. In the intervening months he had travelled across the former Soviet Union, showing the investigators where and how he had killed his victims, using a mannequin and a wooden knife. Then he was examined at the Serbsky Psychiatric Institute in Moscow, infamous in the past for declaring dissidents insane and confining them to mental hospitals. The staff concluded, to his evident surprise, that Chikatilo was legally sane and fit to be tried.

The people of southern Russia had been told only that a man had been charged

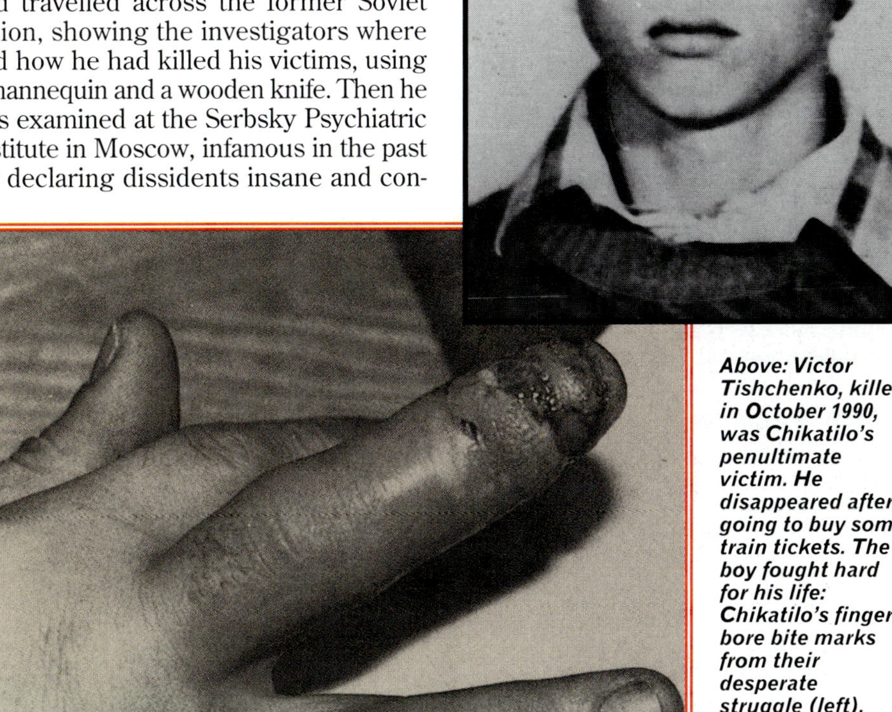

Above: Victor Tishchenko, killed in October 1990, was Chikatilo's penultimate victim. He disappeared after going to buy some train tickets. The boy fought hard for his life: Chikatilo's fingers bore bite marks from their desperate struggle (left).

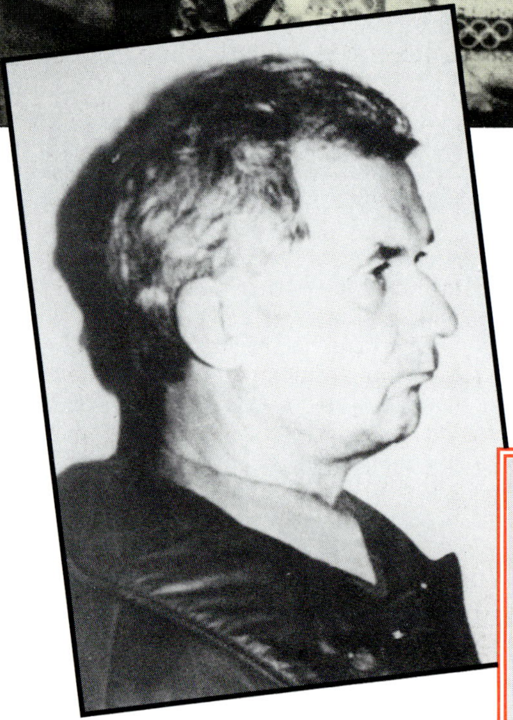

with the killings; he had not been named, and no photograph had been published. Rumours of his activities had spread in Rostov, but for once word of mouth underestimated the truth.

As a result, crowds surged restlessly outside the courtroom at the beginning of the trial, trying to get a glimpse of the man who had terrorised them. There was no room for them; the court was full of journalists from all over the world, experts, witnesses and the relatives of the victims – simple peasants who looked as if they had come in straight from the farm, city-dwellers in sombre suits and ties, and legions of older women in black dresses and headscarves.

Caged like an animal

A metal cage had been built for the accused in a corner of the room. It was guarded by four burly young soldiers, who had a difficult task keeping the spectators at bay as they pressed forward. Chikatilo wore a gaily-coloured shirt, a souvenir of the 1980 Moscow Olympics and his grey hair had been shaved off. This was a prison precaution against head-lice, but had the effect of making Chikatilo look more menacing, more monstrous and more mad.

With the court sitting only three hours a day, it took Judge Leonid Akubzhanov three days to read the charges: 53 counts of murder (two cases had been dropped because no bodies could be found) and

Chikatilo was arrested on 20 November 1990. He was wearing a coat, a black mock-leather cap, and was carrying a large black briefcase which contained two lengths of rope, a pocket mirror and a kitchen knife with a nine-inch blade. The fact that Chikatilo's sperm was of a different group from his blood – an extremely rare phenomenon – meant that he had been eliminated from the murder investigation for many years.

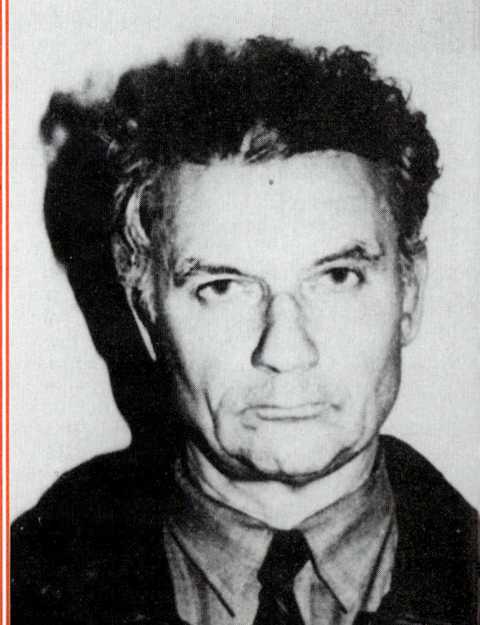

Left: After his arrest Chikatilo seemed indifferent and continued to deny everything. But by the eighth day Chief Inspector Kosteyev thought his prisoner was ready to crack. When he finally did, Chikatilo requested that his interrogators did "not torment me with details and specifics".

several more of child molestation. As he detailed the killings in a flat, legalistic drone, several people in the court fainted, including two of the soldiers guarding the prisoner.

When giving evidence, Chikatilo remained cool and detached, dispassionately describing how he had found and lured away each of his victims. "I did not need to look for them. Every step I took they were there."

The victims' relatives were a different matter. For some, time had dulled the pain; others were too distressed to give evidence at all, but sat in the witness box and wept. The attitude of most of them was expressed by the aunt of a boy killed near Donleskhoz in 1988. "This trial is just rubbing salt into the wounds of the relatives of the victims," she screamed. "We should stop all this and just liquidate the criminal. Too much money is being spent on supporting his life."

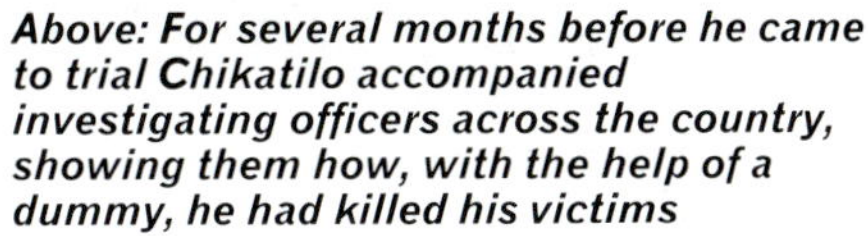

Above: For several months before he came to trial Chikatilo accompanied investigating officers across the country, showing them how, with the help of a dummy, he had killed his victims

The circus atmosphere surrounding the trial waned as the weeks went by. Chikatilo began to use diversionary tactics to whip up more press interest. He would ignore the judge, who is responsible at a Russian trial both for leading the questioning and for giving the verdict, and took to shouting at witnesses. More than once he was dragged downstairs and beaten by his guards, but he could not be subdued.

At one stage he suddenly withdrew his confession to six of the killings. If he had simply denied all the killings, he could be lying to save his skin. By repudiating just six, he succeeded in suggesting that the local police were using him to clear some unsolved murders from their books.

The test that failed

Semen samples had been taken from some of the victims. At this time, before the age of genetic fingerprinting, all that these could reveal was the killer's blood type. All were type AB. A sample of Chikatilo's blood was taken for comparison. It was A. Reluctantly, the police eliminated him from the enquiry. As a result, whenever his name came up as part of the investigation in future, he was discounted.

A few years later, Japanese scientists discovered that a tiny minority of men, perhaps as few as one in a million, were 'paradoxical secretors': their semen was of a different type to their blood group. Unfortunately, none of the officers who had dealt with Chikatilo saw the research and realised its implications.

When Chikatilo was arrested in 1990, samples of both blood and semen were taken, which showed he was a rare paradoxical secretor.

A farcical trial

With most of the important witnesses heard, the mood changed from high drama to farce. Chikatilo, Ukrainian by birth, demanded an interpreter, even though he had a university degree in Russian. His request was overruled. Later, he caused consternation by pulling down his trousers and shouting: "Look at this useless thing. What could I do with that?" This earned him a few days of being barred from the courtroom and a serious beating. When he returned he was handcuffed, and remained that way for the rest of the trial.

His mood swung alarmingly. Sometimes he was almost boisterous, and at

DAILY EXPRESS Thursday October 15 1992

Let me tear Ripper

Woman screams at caged serial killer facing court

From WILL STEWART in Moscow

THE WORLD'S worst serial killer was facing execution last night after being convicted of 52 horrifying murders.

Andrei Chikatilo ranted defiantly through the bars of his courtroom cage as relatives of his victims wept and comforted each other in the public gallery.

...ourning woman dressed ...houted: "Let me tear ...ith my own hands. ...athe the same air ...live on th...

between eight and 16, another 14 girls aged nine to 17, and 17 women, burying most of them in woodland.

But he managed to avoid being caught for 12 years.

Judge Leonid Akubzhanov, who declared the defendant sane, painted a picture of a man dominated by his wife ...hildren.

Right: As the story of Chikatilo's gruesome crimes unfolded, victims' relatives broke down. When they heard how their sons and daughters had been raped, tortured and mutilated, some of them screamed abuse at Chikatilo; others wanted to tear him limb from limb (above).

Rolling his eyes and grimacing, the shaven-headed Chikatilo looked like an inmate of a mental ward. Press photographers ensured that this grotesque image was flashed around the world.

others he did not seem to be following what was going on at all, but sat in his cage slack-jawed or grimacing. When asked a question, he would often answer a completely different enquiry.

In August the lawyers began summing up. When the defence counsel began to speak, Chikatilo got to his feet and began to tunelessly bellow his way through *The Internationale*. He was taken below.

Relative's revenge

Eventually, the judge and his two advisors retired to consider the verdict. The brother of a girl killed by Chikatilo in 1984 tried to save them the trouble. As they filed out he leapt to his feet, pulled a heavy steel ball from his pocket and hurled it at Chikatilo's head. The missile clanged against the railings, whistled past Chikatilo's ear and hit the wall behind his head.

As the guards moved in to make an arrest, others on the public benches formed a protective circle round the white-faced, shaking man. The commander of the guards hesitated for a moment, then waved his hand, and the man was ushered away to safety.

There was to be no such mercy for Chikatilo. After two months – the delay caused by Russia's labyrinthine bureau-

apart

conviction, Chikatilo will learn whether he faces a bul- let in the back of the neck, th usual death penalty in Russi yesterday's hearin

Right: Chikatilo spent the trial incarcerated in a metal cage. When giving evidence he remained cool and detached, but as the weeks went by he started shouting down witnesses. Every minute he delayed or disrupted the trial was another minute of life for him.

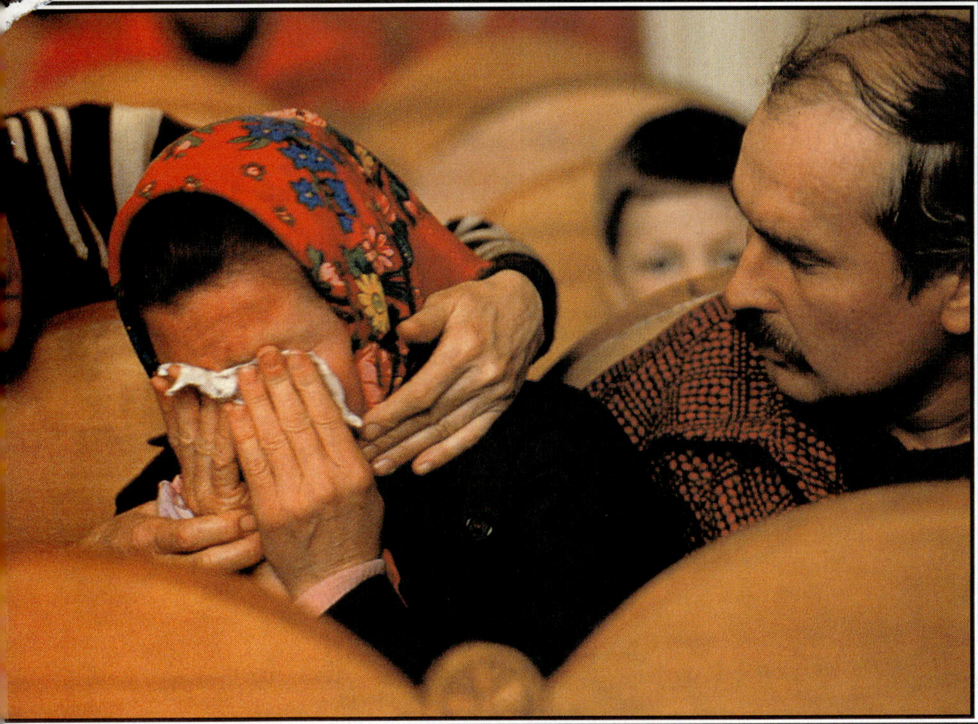

cracy – the court reassembled to hear the judge's verdict.

Ten fully-armed soldiers stood around the cage as Chikatilo was brought in. Stooped and thin, with his hair growing back, he looked more pathetic than monstrous. He sat looking at the floor and trembling slightly. He appeared to have been drugged.

When the judge began to read his verdict, though, he sprang to life. He withdrew his confessions, claimed he had to see a doctor, and then spiralled off into fantasy, saying he had fought in Afghanistan and helped to clean up after Chernobyl.

The small group of victims' relatives, 20 in all, replied by screaming back that he did not deserve a trial. Akubzhanov ordered Chikatilo be taken downstairs, then announced that the defendant had been found guilty of 52 of the killings with which he was charged. He read out the explanation of his verdict, as the law required, in numbing detail. It was the next afternoon before he reached the sentence.

On this occasion the court officials simply let everyone in. The judge had to fight his way to his place in the court. Chikatilo was summoned again, and came up the stairs shouting. The judge just raised his voice and carried on reading.

When he pronounced the death sentence the crowd surged and began to cheer. Chikatilo called him a swindler, snarled and spat. A guard grabbed him by the throat and he was dragged down for the last time, kicking and screaming.

The custom in Russia is not to set a public date for execution. Some time after all the appeals have been exhausted, a team of men come without warning to take the prisoner from the condemned cell to another room, where he is forced to his knees. His indictment and sentence is then read out as the executioner steps up behind him and shoots him in the back of the head with a 9-mm pistol.

Andrei Chikatilo was executed early in 1994.

NEST ISSUE:

Alice Crimmins "I Didn't Kill My Babies"

Right: A resounding cheer filled the courtroom when Judge Akubzhanov announced the death sentence. Chikatilo, snarling like a cornered animal, was grabbed by the throat and dragged kicking and screaming down below for the last time.

MURDER IN HOLLYWOOD

Scandals were rife during Hollywood's heyday. But the furore caused by the shooting of top director William Desmond Taylor in 1922 shook Tinseltown to its very foundations.

Above: Hollywood director William Desmond Taylor's death made headline news across America, sharing the front pages with the trial of screen comedian Fatty Arbuckle for the rape and murder of a young actress.

The courtyard development at 404 Alvarado Street reflected the wealth of the film colony that had, in little more than 10 years, transformed Hollywood from a farming community full of orange groves to one of the most desirable pieces of real estate in the United States. The opulent two-storey stucco buildings – confusingly called bungalows – that clustered around a central garden were home to several film stars, including Charlie Chaplin's leading lady, Edna Purviance.

In 'Bungalow B' lived William Desmond Taylor, a dashing middle-aged English director who had recently been elected President of the Motion Picture Directors' Association.

At just after 7.30 a.m. on 2 February 1922 Henry Peavey, a rather camp black man who acted as Taylor's valet-cum-butler, rushed out of Bungalow B shouting: "The master's dead! The master's dead!" The inhabitants of the courtyard ran into the bungalow and found Taylor sprawled on the floor in the living room.

Crowded scene

News of the director's death spread quickly through the close-knit film colony, and when the police arrived, at about eight o'clock, there were a number of people standing in and around the bungalow. Others came and went in the next hour or so, and some removed articles from the house; but the police did nothing to stop them.

One of the people at the house told the police that a passing doctor had certified that the director had died of natural causes – a stomach haemorrhage. This doctor was never traced, and probably never existed.

When the coroner arrived, at around 9.30, he turned the body over and found a bullet hole in its back. Further investigation revealed that a single shot from a Smith & Wesson .38 had passed through Taylor's lungs and embedded itself in the front of his throat, just below the skin. The angle of the wound, and its alignment with the holes in his clothing, suggested that

Also, several people had seen actress Mabel Normand at the bungalow earlier in the evening.

Twenty-three-year-old Mabel had come from New York to Hollywood in 1915 to join Mack Sennett's Keystone Company. She was an accomplished comedienne, and had appeared with Charlie Chaplin in several films. When Normand was questioned, she confirmed that she had arrived some time after 7 p.m. to borrow a book – Freud's *Inhibition, Symptom and Desire*. Taylor had taken her under his wing, and was helping her to educate herself. He had also been instrumental in persuading her to seek a cure for her cocaine addiction.

When she arrived at the bungalow, she said, the door had been open, despite the chilly weather. Taylor had greeted her, they had chatted for a while, and then he had seen her to her car, parked at the front on Alvarado Street. Normand's chauffeur confirmed her story, and the police ruled her out as a suspect. However, her name continued to be linked to the shooting in the press. Several cinemas refused to show her films, and the scandal was the beginning of the end for her career.

The police found little forensic evidence at the murder scene; so many people had gone in and out in the two hours after the body was found that it would have been of little use even if they had. They decided to look at possible motives, and newspaper columnists and rumour-mongers gleefully joined in.

Drug pusher's revenge?

Theft was immediately ruled out; cash and jewellery were lying in plain view. There was speculation that dope pushers were involved. Taylor had spoken out publicly against drugs. Cocaine fuelled the frenetic creativity and partying of much of early Hollywood, and just about every studio had some shadowy figure hawking heroin, usually as a hangover cure. Could an aggrieved pusher have taken his revenge on the director?

There was also a theory that Taylor had been killed by a wronged husband. The director knew many attractive young actresses, and rumours suggested he was

This cutaway drawing of Taylor's home at 404 Alvarado Street shows the position of the director's body when police arrived. It was only when the coroner turned the corpse over that it was discovered he had been shot.

he had been shot from close range while holding his hands in the air.

Neighbours said they had heard something that might have been a shot at about 7.45 the previous evening, and one of them had seen a muffled figure wearing a long coat and with a "strange walk" leaving Bungalow B at around the same time.

Right: Mabel Normand, the diminutive comedienne, became a major Hollywood star in 1916, making 16 films in five years. Successive scandals put paid to her career and she died in 1930 from tuberculosis, which was probably aggravated by her long-term cocaine addiction.

Biography

Rocky road to fame

The studio biography of William Desmond Taylor insisted he was an English aristocrat who, after a youth of colourful adventuring and stage acting, had gone to Hollywood in 1914 to take the title role in the popular movie, *Captain Alvarez*.

In fact, he was born William Deane Tanner in County Waterford in 1867, the son of an Irish nationalist who was a sergeant in the British Army.

The young William ran away to join a theatre troupe, but was found and brought home. His rebellious streak remained, though, and he and his younger brother Dennis were sent to America, to a school in Kansas that specialised in taming unruly teenagers. Both brothers fell in love with the States and returned there as soon as they were able to leave Ireland for good.

Big break on Broadway

Tanner built up an acting career on Broadway, and in 1901 married an actress, Ethel May Harrison. Her wealthy father set up the newly-weds by buying into the English Antique Shop on New York's 5th Avenue and making Tanner manager and part-owner.

The couple had a daughter, Daisy Deane Tanner, in 1903, but cracks were appearing in the relationship. Tanner had had a number of homosexual affairs in his youth, and found it difficult to maintain a sexual relationship with his wife. He began drinking heavily, and on 23 October 1908 walked out of the shop and effectively disappeared.

He drifted around the country doing odd jobs before returning to the stage in San Francisco, where he was recruited to star, under his new name, as Captain Alvarez. At 47 he was a little too old to get any more romantic leads, and he turned to directing, working mainly on short features and serials.

His former wife – she had divorced him and remarried four years after his desertion – recognised him in 1917 when she saw *Captain Alvarez*. They never met again, but he paid for his daughter's education and was reconciled with Daisy the year before he died.

Homosexuality kept secret

The suave, handsome man with the elegant English accent had many admirers among female Hollywood stars, including Mary Miles Minter and Mabel Normand, but by this time Taylor had given up all pretence of bisexuality, although he was very discreet about his personal life. The studio bosses, though, knew he was gay, and it was evidence of this – rather than of amorous liaisons with female stars – that they were keen on removing from the house after his death. Stories of his prodigious appetite for young women helped cover up their trail.

One clue escaped their attention, however. The mysterious bunch of keys at the murder house belonged to a rented flat. There Taylor met young men procured for him by Henry Peavey, who had been set to appear in court on an indecency charge the day that he found Taylor's body.

Below: A gun-totin' Taylor starred in **Captain Alvarez**, *his first big-screen film which was made in 1914.*

more than friendly with some of them. The police had found bundles of letters in the house from, among others, Mabel Normand and Mary Miles Minter, another popular young actress. They were all essentially innocent, if occasionally flirtatious, but suggested that the dead man had a fatal attractiveness for women.

It was also widely reported that a pink silk nightgown, embroidered with the letters MMM, had been found in one of the bedrooms. Mary Miles Minter was interviewed and denied any knowledge of the nightgown. She said she had been at home, reading to other members of her family, on the night Taylor was killed. Mary's mother, Charlotte Selby, her grandmother and her sister all confirmed this.

Blackmail theory

The most widely-accepted motive was that Taylor had been killed by a blackmailer, either in an argument over payment or because he threatened to go to the police. One fact which suggested blackmail was that Taylor had withdrawn $2,300 – a large amount of money in those days – from his bank account a couple of days before his death, and had paid it back in on the day he was killed. Although it was later revealed that Taylor had taken out the money to buy a present for Mabel Normand and had replaced it when he found he could not get what he wanted, the blackmail theory persisted.

Police suspicion fell on a man named Edward Sands, who had been taken on by

Right: Henry Peavey, Taylor's butler who found his employer dead, had been arrested for soliciting young men. But it was never established whether he was working on his own or under orders from his master.

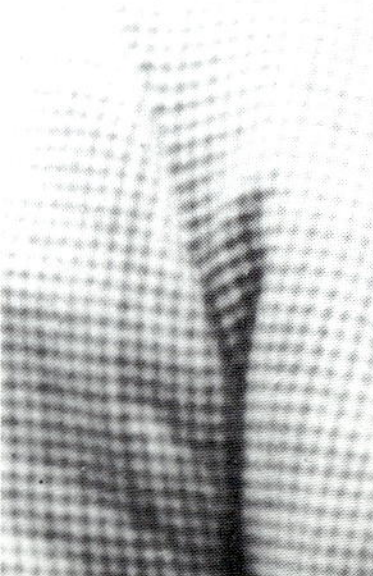

Around 30,000 people turned out for Taylor's garish funeral on 13 February 1922. At one point Mary Miles Minter threw herself at Taylor's open coffin and kissed the corpse full on the lips. She then caused a stir by announcing that it had spoken. "He whispered to me, it sounded like 'I shall love you always Mary'," said the actress.

Taylor as a chauffeur and secretary a couple of years earlier. Taylor had gone on holiday to Europe in July 1921, leaving Sands in charge of the bungalow. But when Taylor returned he found that his house had been ransacked. Sands had taken clothes, jewellery and $2,400 in cash, and made his escape in Taylor's Packard Roadster. Cheque books were also missing, and scraps of paper in the waste basket showed that the chauffeur had been practising Taylor's signature; more than $5,000 had been taken from his account.

Main suspect disappears

The car was soon found, wrecked, on the other side of Los Angeles, but there was no trace of Sands. A few weeks later a letter arrived at Alvarado Street, addressed to William Deane Tanner (Taylor's real name, which he kept very quiet). In it were several pawn tickets, which allowed Taylor to redeem some cherished trinkets.

Despite his loss and betrayal, Taylor had refused to press charges against Sands, which suggested that the chauffeur had some kind of hold over him. There was also some speculation that he was, in fact, Taylor's brother – he certainly seemed to know a lot about him. A countrywide search for Edward Sands was ordered.

In the meantime, police concentrated on some confusing sightings of suspicious men in the vicinity of the house on the night of the murder, but these led nowhere. In addition, several booze suppliers were interviewed after a woman reported overhearing a quarrel about drink the night before the murder. No-one was charged.

The investigation gradually wound down, although the files remained open. Then, in 1926, a new District Attorney took over the case. He soon established that Charlotte Selby had not been listening to her daughter Mary Miles Minter read on the night of the murder. But when Charlotte was questioned she came up with another alibi, which was confirmed by two men – a friend and a night-watchman. The District Attorney seemed satisfied.

Starlet involved

Edward Sands remained the official number one suspect. However, the police apparently had very strong evidence that he had committed suicide in Darien, Connecticut, a few weeks after Taylor died. And rumours around Hollywood continued to suggest that Mary Miles Minter and her mother, Charlotte Selby, were somehow involved. The image of the pink nightgown had burned itself on the public consciousness, and it had become widely known that Charlotte had owned a Smith & Wesson pistol in 1920. She had several times threatened Mary's would-be suitors with it.

As a result of these rumours, Selby and Minter jointly applied in 1937 to the then District Attorney, Buron Fitts, to produce any material evidence he had linking them

Actress Mabel Normand, seen here with the District Attorney and his assistant, admitted that she had visited Taylor on the night of his death to pick up a book.

Left: Mary Miles Minter made her film debut at the age of 12, when her blue eyes and golden curls were in great demand. After six films she went to the Flying Studio in Santa Barbara, where she met and worked with William Desmond Taylor. Both of them then moved to Paramount, where Minter was groomed to succeed Mary Pickford as 'America's Sweetheart'. But she became disenchanted with acting and fought continuously with her domineering mother.

Edward F. Sands, Taylor's former chauffeur and secretary, was the number one suspect in the murder case because he had previously stolen cash and jewellery from Taylor and forged his signature. He also knew details of his employer's murky private life.

with the crime, or to publicly exonerate them. Fitts was content to clear their names, and the murder remains on the police books as unsolved.

The Taylor case became one of the most famous of all murder mysteries. In 1967 one of Taylor's contemporaries, veteran director King Vidor, began researching it for a screenplay that he hoped would resuscitate his career. He interviewed the surviving participants, and dug deep into official and unofficial records.

The film was never made, but Vidor discovered some interesting new evidence. His findings, however, were not published until 1986, after his biographer, Sidney Kirkpatrick, found a cache of papers in a strongbox after Vidor's death. Beneath clouds of disinformation, much of it put out by studio bosses for their own purposes, the director's research uncovered a fairly simple case. The killer's identity had been protected by three successive District Attorneys – for money.

As the case was officially still open the police records were not available for public scrutiny, but Vidor had a contact in the Los Angeles Police Department who allowed him to see them. They revealed that much of the press speculation about the case was wildly ill-founded, and that the police had hard evidence which they had never made public.

Three long blonde hairs, found on the jacket Taylor was wearing when he died, belonged to Mary Miles Minter. There was also testimony that Charlotte Selby, Mary's mother, had been actively looking for her daughter not long before the murder, and that she had telephoned someone with the news of Taylor's death before 7.30 on the morning the body was discovered. In fact, all the suppressed evidence threw suspicion on Minter and Selby.

Bribed to keep quiet

Vidor tracked down a detective who had interviewed Margaret Selby, Mary's sister, in 1937, at a time when the whole family was involved in various lawsuits concerning the family fortune – largely what Mary had earned in her short acting career. During one of these cases an accountant testified that money that had gone missing from Mary's account had been siphoned off by Charlotte to pay off the District Attorneys to keep her out of the Taylor case.

Margaret Selby's story was that, on the night of the murder, Mary had fought with her mother about her (basically unrequited) passion for Taylor and had been locked in her room. She had got out and rushed off to Taylor's house, arriving just before Mabel Normand. Minter had hid upstairs during Mabel's visit.

When Charlotte Selby realised she was gone, she had made a few phone calls and then hurried over to Alvarado Street. While Taylor was seeing Mabel to her car, Selby had slipped into the house through the open front door, intending to confront Taylor and insist, at gunpoint, that he left her daughter alone. Her concern was not so much for Mary's virtue, which was dubious, as for the fact that her meal ticket might find another home. There was also a suggestion that Charlotte was herself romantically interested in Taylor.

The first thing Selby saw as she entered the house was Mary coming down the stairs from the bedroom. Outraged, she pulled her gun on Taylor as he came back into the house, and killed him.

Margaret's story was backed up by hard evidence. Though the murder weapon had been tossed into a swamp by Charlotte's mother in the summer of 1922, the police had some spent bullets, taken from Charlotte Selby's practice range in the basement of her home, to compare with the one taken from Taylor's body.

Was Selby the killer?

Charlotte Selby, however, was still not indicted. Every time new evidence came up, she paid officials to suppress it. When she challenged Buron Fitts to charge or exonerate her, she coupled this with a once-and-for-all pay-off to lose all the physical evidence linking her to the case. This included the murder weapon, dragged from a swamp near the Miles family plantation in Louisiana.

Although it was never proved that Charlotte Selby murdered William Desmond Taylor, King Vidor's theory was the most convincing of all those put forward.

Forty-five years after Taylor's murder director King Vidor (right) researched the crime in order to make it into a film. He managed to track down Mary Miles Minter, whom he remembered as a beautiful young actress but was now a haggard, obese old woman. When he explained his murder theory to her, she snapped: "You don't know anything about it. Mr Taylor was a great man." But when pressed on the point, she sobbed: "My mother killed everything I ever loved."

Scandal city

Although not the finely-tuned gossip machine it became in the 1930s and 1940s, Hollywood in the early 1920s was a hotbed of scandal and rumour. Newspaper magnates like William Randolph Hearst had already learned that stories about stars – especially those involving sex, bootleg liquor and drugs – sold newspapers.

Raunchy rumours

Among the half-truths and fabrications widely reported at the time were that Taylor's body had been neatly laid out on the carpet; that police had arrived to find movie mogul Adolph Zukor and Mabel Normand searching through the dead man's papers and burning some in the living-room fireplace; that a search of the house had discovered a locked closet full of female underwear, all neatly tagged with initials and dates, that were widely assumed to be souvenirs of conquests; that there was a cache of pornographic photographs featuring Taylor with several actresses; that a huge bunch of keys found at the scene opened many famous bedroom doors; and that Taylor had trafficked bootleg liquor and/or drugs.

Some of these rumours were founded in fact, but most were deliberately invented or exaggerated by studios and newspapers for their own ends; Taylor's studio Paramount, for instance, had compelling reasons for making him sound like a dashing Lothario – he was in fact homosexual.

Paramount Studios (right) worked hard at covering up Taylor's private life – the last thing they wanted was another sex scandal.

A DOUBLE KILLING

Most people who noticed two young women slumped in a parked car in a quiet north London street thought they were sleeping off a night on the town. But they were in fact dead, the victims of a brutal killer.

A gold-coloured Toyota Corolla was neatly parked beside the kerb. There were two women slumped inside it, one in the front passenger seat, the other in the back.

To people hurrying along Spears Road in Holloway, north London, on the morning of 23 July 1990, the women appeared to be fast asleep. But when workers started arriving at the small factories dotted along the road they became concerned. One factory worker tried the door handles, but the car was locked. The two occupants were not stirring at all, and they did not seem to be breathing. A member of the public called the police.

When the officers arrived at the scene they knocked on the car windows, but still the women remained deathly still. Detec-

The bodies of Elaine Forsyth (left) and Patricia Morrison (above) were found inside a Toyota Corolla, parked a few hundred yards from their north London flat. Both had been strangled with two separate ligatures. Police examined the car (main picture) after they received a call from a local factory worker who suspected that the women were dead.

tives were called, and a door was prised open using a wire coat-hanger.

The women were dead. One appeared to have been strangled with a leather strap still taut around her neck, but there were no other signs of violence in the car. The detectives called the Area Major Incident Pool at Edmonton police station and asked for specialist help. A double murder investigation was launched.

Victims identified

The victims were quickly identified as Patricia Morrison, aged 28, and 31-year-old Elaine Forsyth. Both women worked for the same firm of estate agents and they shared a flat together in Grenville Road, less than a mile from where their bodies were found. The 'B' registered Toyota belonged to Patricia; her friend was only a learner driver.

Patricia Morrison was in the back of the car, and although she was dressed only in a bra and summer shorts, there were no signs of sexual assault. Her friend Elaine was wearing a T-shirt and jeans, and she had not been molested either.

Detective Superintendent Geoff Parratt, one of Scotland Yard's most experienced murder investigators, quickly took in the known facts. His concluded that both women must have been killed elsewhere and their bodies put in the car. The killer must then have driven the car to where it was found.

A post-mortem examination showed that the victims had been strangled, and death had probably occurred about 36 hours before, on Saturday 21 July. Pathologist Dr Vensa Djorovic said that Patricia had been strangled with a leather handbag strap which was still round her neck when she was found, and that her killer had approached her from the front.

Her friend Elaine had been grabbed from behind, and a curtain tie found at the flat was the ligature used to kill her. She had fought strongly and had probably taken more than a minute to die.

There were vital things that Parratt and his team needed to know quickly, including details of the women's friends. Parratt already had a hunch that the women had been killed by someone they knew. But what was the motive?

Details of the murders were released to the media. Information started coming in, and the murder squad moved methodically ahead. While one team of detectives carefully searched the dead women's flat, others concentrated on their diaries and address books. The flat showed signs of a struggle, which was consistent with what the CID already knew. The women, who had multiple bruising, had obviously fought fiercely for their lives.

When questioned, neighbours said they had heard sounds of screaming and fighting coming from the flat on the Saturday evening, 21 July, but had dismissed it as a domestic fight between the two women. One of them spoke of hearing a series of bumping sounds, like something being dragged past a radiator.

It looked very much as if Patricia and Elaine had been attacked in their own flat. This was confirmed when blood splashes were found on the floor and skirting board in the hallway. The bumping sound was probably the noise of the killer taking his victims' bodies down the stairs.

According to information given to the detectives, there had been a length of carpet in the hallway. Now it was missing. What had happened to it? Again Parratt thought he already knew the answer. The killer had probably got rid of the carpet because there was blood on it.

The press appeals were also bearing fruit. A few hours after news of the killings broke, the police were approached by 34-year-old Michael Shorey.

Ex-lover questioned

Shorey, who worked as an accounts clerk for a London advertising agency, had been Elaine's lover on and off for about eight years; they had even become engaged and had planned to marry. But earlier that summer the relationship had

Right: Detective Superintendent Geoff Parratt, heading the murder enquiry, thought it was likely the girls had been killed by someone they knew. An examination of the flat revealed that a struggle had taken place there, but provided no clues as to the motive for the murders.

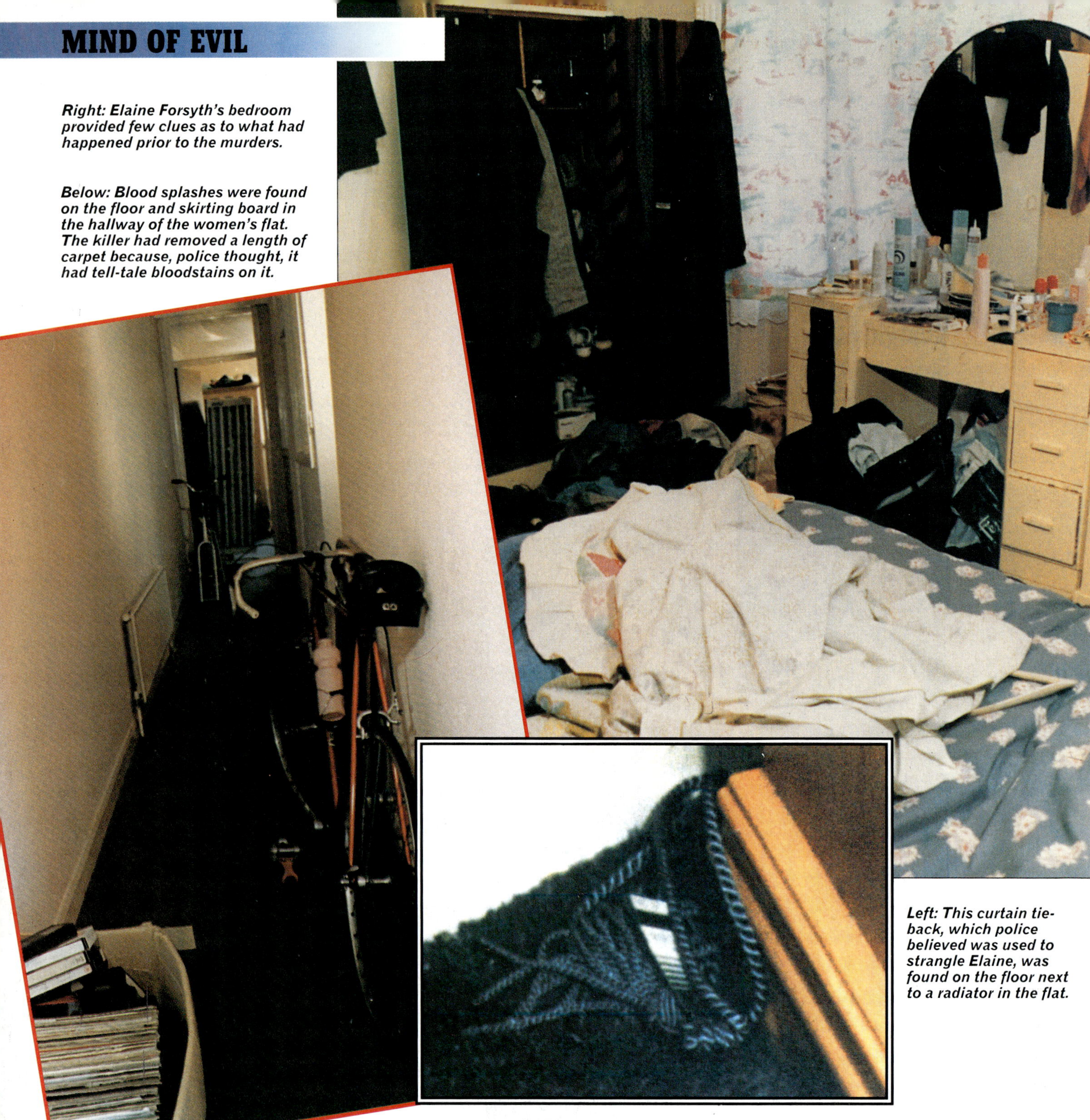

Right: Elaine Forsyth's bedroom provided few clues as to what had happened prior to the murders.

Below: Blood splashes were found on the floor and skirting board in the hallway of the women's flat. The killer had removed a length of carpet because, police thought, it had tell-tale bloodstains on it.

Left: This curtain tie-back, which police believed was used to strangle Elaine, was found on the floor next to a radiator in the flat.

cooled and the couple stopped seeing each other.

The accounts clerk denied harming either of the women, but Parratt and his colleagues were suspicious. Shorey said he had an alibi – he had spent the whole weekend with his new lover.

His girlfriend confirmed that Shorey had been with her when scientific evidence indicated Elaine and Patricia were being killed. But Parratt and his right-hand man, Detective Inspector Graham Lillington, were not convinced. Shorey seemed too cool. Although he appeared distraught to the officers, it looked as if it was feigned.

And there was something else they knew: Shorey already had a terrible history of violence and cruelty towards women.

Violent past

Several years earlier he lived with a woman who had a nine-year-old daughter. When the child annoyed him he had deliberately dipped her feet into a bowl of boiling water. The child required plastic surgery, and Shorey was jailed. He had later been in trouble again for a series of assaults on another lover, which ended with him piercing her arms and legs with darts and stabbing her with a javelin. The woman also talked of being whipped by Shorey with a car aerial while she was seven months pregnant. But none of this was evidence of murder.

After 30 hours of questioning he was released; Shorey appeared to be in the clear. To the outside world the case seemed to have become bogged down. The only course was for the murder squad to follow every available lead to prove what they really believed, that the suave young man with shoulder-length black hair was a double murderer who thought he was going to get away with it.

Press appeals about the Toyota car were highly productive. Dozens of witnesses contacted the incident room and police were quickly able to build up a picture which indicated that the dead women had been driven around or left parked in the

the two women slumped inside. People said they had not called the police because they did not suspect anything was amiss. Their explanations ranged from: "I thought they were asleep," to "I thought they were flat out from drink," to "They looked like they'd been doing drugs." One witness even spoke of a group of young men rocking the car and banging on the windows, then moving on when they got no response.

Below: Michael Shorey went to the police on the morning after the bodies were discovered. He immediately aroused suspicion by giving conflicting answers during questioning. Police said he gave four different versions of when he had last seen the women, and failed to show any sign of the grief expected after hearing of the death of a girlfriend he once planned to marry.

But the most interesting sightings were from on the day the bodies were found. Several early-morning motorists called to say that they had seen the Toyota with the two motionless women slumped in it travelling along Junction Road, Holloway, at the start of the morning rush hour. The car was being driven in such a slow and erratic fashion that it got in the way of other traffic. Several of them spoke of the driver either being "drunk" or "not used to the car". One man had even hooted and gesticulated at the driver to get out of the way. He gave a detailed description of the driver to the police: he was a young black man with long permed hair.

Important evidence

The detectives were very interested to hear this. Michael Shorey had been born in Barbados, and had long permed hair. In itself Parratt and his team knew it still wasn't quite enough. They thought they

area for up to 24 hours before they were found.

On the morning of Sunday 22 July the car was seen parked in Ronalds Road, Holloway. It later disappeared, only to reappear at the same location several hours later. There was no doubt that the witnesses were correct; all spoke of seeing

Right: Gary MacRae, a former friend of Shorey, provided police with the hard evidence they needed to secure a conviction. He said Michael Shorey had asked him to look after a carpet on Sunday 22 July – the day before the dead girls were found

LIFE FOR THE BODIES IN CAR KILLER

By PAUL HENDERSON

EVIL strangler Michael Shorey sobbed uncontrollably yesterday as he was jailed for life for the 'bodies-in-the-car' murders of two career girls.

After the Old Bailey verdi the father of one of Shore victims, his girlfriend E Forsyth, spoke of his de the waste of her life.

Above: Shorey's sentencing made front-page news. The jury of eight women and four men, after deliberating for more than seven hours, returned a unanimous verdict of guilty of both murders at the end of the 16-day trial.

Above: Michael Storey, handcuffed to a prison guard, is led away from the Old Bailey to begin his life sentence for the brutal killing of the two estate agents.

ISBN 1-85875-028-8
9 781858 750286

had pieced together most of the jigsaw, but they needed one really strong piece of evidence. A few days later they found it.

A vital clue

Gary MacRae, a friend of Michael Shorey, rang the murder incident room; he wanted to talk to detectives urgently. He said that on 22 July Shorey had contacted him and asked if he would look after something. Shorey brought the item round wrapped inside a plastic dustbin liner. When MacRae asked him what was inside, Shorey had replied: "It's a carpet." The next day MacRae heard about the murders, and now he wanted to tell his story to the police.

Detectives opened up the bag and found a nine-foot length of carpet inside. It was the piece missing from the hall at Elaine and Patricia's flat. At Scotland Yard's forensic labs in Lambeth, scientists soon found what they were looking for. There were spots of blood and saliva soaked into the pile, and the blood matched that of the dead women.

For five weeks the police were content to allow the world, and Shorey, to think the trail had gone cold, while in total secrecy they assembled their armoury of evidence. Then, on 4 September, they raided Shorey's flat in nearby Crouch End. They found him in bed with yet another woman. He was arrested, questioned and charged with double murder.

Shorey denies murders

Michael Shorey went on trial at the Old Bailey on 11 June 1991. He denied both murders. Prosecuting counsel Michael Nutting told the jury that Shorey had strangled Elaine after a row about their relationship, which had gone wrong. He told the court: "He then strangled her friend Patricia because she had either found out what he had done or to stop her finding out."

But Shorey stuck to his story that he was with his girlfriend throughout the fatal weekend. She in turn backed this up, saying he had been with her at her flat from the Saturday afternoon.

The jury heard police evidence that during questioning Shorey had changed the details about his movements on the weekend in question four times. When he was asked why he had asked a friend to look after the bloodstained carpet, he had denied knowing the man.

There was one more piece of deadly scientific evidence against Shorey. A pair of trainers he had worn that weekend were found to have tiny traces of blood belonging to the dead women on them. It had dripped onto his heels as he slung their bodies over his shoulder to carry them outside to the car.

The trial ended on 3 July, when the jury returned an unanimous verdict of guilty to both murders. Michael Shorey was jailed for life.

NEXT ISSUE:
Killed For Their Cash